Do You Want To Play?

A Book About
BEING FRIENDS

Bob Kolar

Dutton Children's Books   New York

for
Jonathan
and
Nicholas

The tiny line figures that appear throughout the book greet each other
with *hello* in the following languages (in order of appearance): English, French,
Swahili, Japanese, Russian, Spanish, Italian, German, Portuguese, Chinese, Polish,
Dutch, Hebrew, and Hindi. On the doormats, the word *welcome* appears in
English, Swahili, German, Dutch, French, Chinese, Japanese, English, and Russian.

Copyright © 1999 by Bob Kolar
All rights reserved.
CIP Data is available.
Published in the United States 1999 by Dutton Children's Books,
a division of Penguin Putnam Books for Young Readers
345 Hudson Street, New York, New York 10014
http://www.penguinputnam.com/yreaders/index.htm
Typography designed by Sara Reynolds and Richard Amari
Printed in Hong Kong
First Edition   10 9 8 7 6 5 4 3 2 1
ISBN 0-525-45938-3

The artwork for this book was created by collage, using various colored
tissue and handmade papers and all sorts of miscellaneous scraps.
Detail was painted in gouache and ink.

Hi! Do you want to play?
I know a great place.

Sure! I'm ready for anything.

WILD AMAZING ADVENTURES

HEP, 2, 3, 4, HEP, 2, 3, 4 . . .

Nice dots.

Nice pots.

Maybe I'll meet someone new.

I hope it's a big show.

I'll take it from here. We've been saving the best seats for you.

Where's the popcorn?

How does my hair look?

IT'S JUST FINE. LET'S HURRY UP.

Watch out! Don't slip!

GOOD

SEATS.

AVAILABLE

Everyone here makes
different sounds, and our
sounds together make a song.
Ready now? A-one and a-two and . . .

Toota
Toota
Toota

aarummmmnm

Weezy Squeezy

shakashakashakashaka

shakashakashakashaka

Ratta tat tat Ratta tat tat

swaaa-o o o o

bingo

bingo

bango

bango

bongo

bongo

HONK!

oh, baby!

Twang

Twang

Jambo.

GOOD FRIEND INSTRUCTIONS

SIZE—(a...

EYES—for seeing the world in your own special way (also useful in making funny faces)

EARS—for listening to secrets and stories, feelings and wishes

MOUTH—for saying good things like "Let's be friends" and "Want to play with us?" (also good for blowing bubbles and smiling)

ARMS—for hugging and reaching

BELLY—for enjoying after-school snacks (like jelly and banana sandwiches) with friends

BRAIN—for thinking of friendly stuff like making a picture for someone or playing games together

SILLY HAT—(optional)

NOSE—because you nose a good joke!

Why did the chicken cross the playground?

To get to the other slide!

Where did the general keep his armies?

In his sleevies!

How do you catch a squirrel?

Climb up a tree and act like a nut!

HANDS—for helping and holding (also handy for building snowmen, sand castles, and forts)

LAUGH—must be easy to use (even when a joke's not funny)

HEART—a big one

HA HA HA

Privet.

Just be yourself.

Do we have all this stuff?

This is getting heavy.

FEET—for dancing, of course
(any size will do)

SOCKS—colorful (just kidding—
any kind will do, or none at all)

Let's just play!

Let's not worry about all that stuff.

FRIENDLY TIP #4
Now and then, everybody has stinky feet.

JUMP HIGH

TELL JOKES

BUILD THINGS

PLAY SUPERHEROES

PRETEND

SNACK TIME

PLAY BALL

EXPLORE

SHARE FEELINGS

CLEAN UP

MAKE FACES

PUT ON A SHOW

PLAY BALL AGAIN

SNACK TIME AGAIN

SLEEP OVER

MAKE NOISE

TEASE SOMEONE SMALLER
Go to the Thinking Spot

HUG A FRIEND
Move ahead 4

Uh-oh.

ACT BOSSY
Go to the Thinking Spot

Too bad.

How To Play

1) GET SOME FRIENDS
2) FIND YOUR DICE
3) USE COINS AS MARKERS
4) THE YOUNGEST GOES FIRST
5) FIRST ONE TO REACH THE FINISH IS THE WINNER

NO TURNING

WRITE A LETTER TO A FRIEND
Move ahead 3

STRAIGHT ONLY

STUCK IN STUCK-UP SWAMP
Lose a turn

STICK UP FOR A FRIEND
Take another turn

CALL SOMEONE STUPID
Go to the Thinking Spot

I'm really rolling now!

MAKE A FRIEND SMILE
Move ahead 5

WON'T SHARE
Go back 4

DO THE RIGHT THING
Make a turn only if you land here

HIT SOMEONE
Go to the Thinking Spot

We win!   I'm tired.

MAKE FUN OF SOMEONE
Move back 3

FORGIVE A FRIEND
Move ahead 3

I win!

MAKE A BIRTHDAY CARD
Roll again

QUICK, EASY SHORTCUT

CLOSED

LIE TO A FRIEND
Move back 3

FINISH

READ A BOOK TO A FRIEND
Move ahead 1

INTERMISSION

Hallo.

Grrrr

READ ME NEXT!

Now I want to be by myself and read.

I hope he reads the story out loud.

FRIENDLY TIP #1
If you like someone, tell him or her.
If you don't like them, keep it to yourself.

THE BIG ANGRY BEAR

ONE MORNING, a rabbit and a squirrel were out walking in the forest when they happened upon a big, angry bear.

"Why are you so angry?" asked the rabbit.

"It's much better to be happy," said the squirrel.

"I'm just angry!" growled the bear. "In fact, I'm so angry that I think I shall eat the two of you for lunch."

The two friends knew they were in big trouble. Quickly, the rabbit said, "Dear Bear, it's much too early for a proper lunch. How about if we play some baseball first?"

"Yes," added the squirrel. "I'm sure you're very good at batting the ball."

The big, angry bear was puzzled. He had never played baseball. The forest animals were always afraid to include him. "Well, okay," he said, thinking it might be fun. "But just until lunchtime."

It turned out the big, angry bear was not very good at batting. He swung and he missed, and he swung and he missed, and he got even angrier. "This is stupid!" he said. "Is it lunchtime yet?"

"Oh, not yet," cried the rabbit.

"It won't be lunchtime until you hit a home run," said the squirrel.

But after a long while of watching the bear swing and miss and swing and miss, the two friends could not stand it anymore. So they began to help. "Keep your eye on the ball." "Hold your bat like this." "Wait for a good pitch," they told the bear.

Soon the bear was not only batting the ball, he was having fun. He even hit a home run. "Time for lunch!" he roared.

The two friends were scared. But the bear had liked baseball. The bear had liked hitting a home run. And most of all, the bear had liked having friends to play with. "Rabbit and squirrel," said the bear. "Promise me one thing, and I won't eat you."

"What is that?" they asked.

"Promise me that we can all be friends and play baseball after lunch."

So the rabbit and the squirrel promised, and the three friends went out for a lunch of berries and salad. From that day on, they played lots of baseball, and the bear hit home runs clear to the end of the forest.

T H E   E N D

Hey, I'm back.

I've been waiting.
I missed you.

Don't bug me
I'm reading.

If I moved, we could still be friends.

We could? Hey, that's right!

We can all pedal together, so everyone hop on!
Easy-to-get friends,
Yet-to-be-met friends,
Even faithful pet friends!
Orange friends and blue friends,
How-do-you-do friends,
New and tried-and-true friends.
Bring your kiss-and-hug friends
And don't forget your bug friends.

WE'VE SAVED SOME SEATS FOR OTHERS.

There's room for everyone.

KEEP Going

FRIENDLY TIP #5
Don't tattle unless someone could get hurt.

We've got a whole lot of friends
and plenty of space.
We're all together,
sharing one big place.

VACANCY

237

FRIENDLY TIP #12
If you have something special,
after a while share it (except gum).

Welcome

5

KARIBU

WANT TO PLAY HOUSE?

That's easy.

つの上達の秘けつは、
す。そしておいしく感じる
るか考●みる。可能な
かせてもらったりする。こう
的に上げることができま
楽しさは料理にとって重
生にも得意・不得意があ
ることもあります。そんなと
がとても役に立ちます。そ

414

WILLKOMMEN

Let's hold hands and dance!

WELKOM

104

76

ようこそ

歡迎

Shalom.

Bienvenue

АоБро
пожаловать!

WELCOME

I've put down roots.

Don't be shy. Join in.

I like holding hands.

My arms are stretching!

Wish I could dance.

8

I like to draw.

Draw a picture of me.

Can we stop to get something to eat?

Dig my fancy footwork!

This is making me dizzy.

I can be smart.

I can be anything.

And before we have to part, tell a friend what's in your heart.

I don't want to stop.

You don't have to—there's one more page.

I just want to be LOUD!

This is the last page.   **Do you want to play?**
What do we do now?

Hello again.

see you later, alligator.